MAGIC QUEST

RACE TO THE MAGIC MOUNTAIN

Written by
Bernard Mensah

Art by
Natasha Nayo

BRANCHES

SCHOLASTIC INC.

KWAME'S
MAGIC
QUEST

Read more adventures!

1

2

3

TABLE OF CONTENTS

To all the children (and adults) that dream of African magic, this is for you!—BM

To my family and friends who have always supported me in my artistic journey. Thank you so much for always being my inspiration and my strength.—NN

While Kwame's Magic Quest takes place in a fantasy world, many of the places, people, clothes, names, food, and cultures come from real African countries. The author would like to thank Adjei Kwesi Boateng for sharing his knowledge of Ghanaian culture for this book.

Library of Congress Cataloging-in-Publication Data

Names: Mensah, Bernard (Children's author), author. | Nayo, Natasha, illustrator. Title: Race to the magic mountain / written by Bernard Mensah ; illustrated by Natasha Nayo. Description: First edition. | New York : Branches/Scholastic Inc., 2024. | Series: Kwame's magic quest ; 2 | Audience: Ages 6–8. | Audience: Grades 1–3. | Summary: Eight-year-old Kwame is called upon to save the world from the evil magic that has turned his friend into a green flame—new to magic he has four days to learn as much as he can before setting out on a dangerous journey to the Magic Mountain, where the flame is trying to create an all-powerful calabash. Identifiers: LCCN 2023022976 (print) | ISBN 9781338843316 (paperback) | ISBN 9781338843323 (library binding) Subjects: LCSH: Magic—Juvenile fiction. | Gourds—Juvenile fiction. | Good and evil—Juvenile fiction. | Schools—Juvenile fiction. | Friendship—Juvenile fiction. | Ghana—Juvenile fiction. | CYAC: Magic—Fiction. | Gourds—Fiction. | Good and evil—Fiction. | Schools—Fiction. | Friendship—Fiction. | Ghana—Fiction. | LCGFT: Action and adventure fiction. Classification: LCC PZ7.1.M47326 Rk 2024 (print) | DDC 823.92 [Fic]—dc23/eng/20230516 LC record available at https://lccn.loc.gov/2023022976

10 9 8 7 6 5 4 3 2 1   24 25 26 27 28

Printed in India   197
First edition, August 2024
Edited by Katie Carella
Cover design by Brian LaRossa
Book design by Jaime Lucero

DEAR KWAME,

Welcome back to your magical journey! As you know, I'm the head of Nkonyaa (IN-kohn-YAH) School. Nkonyaa is what we call magic.

Every child comes here when they turn eight years old. When you arrived, you received a magic calabash from the Nkonyaa Tree. But your calabash's magic type was a mystery. At first, it didn't show any of the four magic symbols below.

calabashes

 EARTH BREAKER
These calabashes control soil, rocks, or anything inside the earth.

 SUN WIELDER
These calabashes control fire.

 TIME BENDER
These calabashes control time.

 WEATHER HANDLER
These calabashes control the weather.

Imagine my surprise when we found out your calabash is actually a rare Omni calabash that can perform all four magic types! Only one other person has held an Omni—Okomfo Anochi, the most powerful Nkonyaa elder!

There are four magic levels. At each level, magic gets harder! Right now, you are at the beginner-magic level.

BEGINNER MAGIC	BASIC MAGIC	HALFWAY MAGIC	ADVANCED MAGIC

Kwame, we need your help! The world and magic are in danger. The green flame has escaped with the two most powerful calabashes—the Boni calabash and Okomfo Anochi's Omni calabash. Only you can get them back! Are you ready?

Yours in Magic,

Principal Wari

MEET THE CHARACTERS

Kwame

Fifi

Esi

Papa-Kow

Principal Wari

Baaba

CHAPTER 1

NO TIME TO WASTE

Kwame watched Principal Wari pour brown liquid on the ground. It smelled sweet and sour.

"This liquid is called pito. It's the Earth Spirits' favorite drink," the principal said.

Kwame had only arrived at Nkonyaa School a few days ago. He didn't know much magic yet. But he had just agreed to help save the world!

His friend Fifi had stolen the two most powerful calabashes. The evil Boni calabash had turned Fifi into a green flame. And the flame had escaped with both calabashes. Without these two calabashes safely at the school, the world had started to fall apart!

Kwame gripped his Omni calabash. He had used it to cast a stay-same spell to help keep the world from crumbling. But the spell wouldn't last long... Kwame had to bring the special calabashes back before it was too late!

The pito on the ground bubbled.

"Earth Spirits live inside the earth," Principal Wari explained as he poured out more liquid. "They will know where the green flame is."

The pito bubbled, making strange symbols in the soil. Principal Wari read them.

"What are the spirits saying?" Kwame asked.

"The green flame is headed to the top of the Magic Mountain," Principal Wari replied. "It plans to cast a spell using the power of the mountain. It wants to combine the Boni and Omni calabashes to make one all-powerful calabash. If the evil flame succeeds, it will be too strong to stop. You must reach the mountain before it casts that spell."

Suddenly, smoke came up out of the pito.

Principal Wari raised his eyebrows. "The spirits say they will send you something special to help you on your journey."

Kwame gulped. *I need all the help I can get to reach the mountain and stop the flame from casting that spell!*

NO TIME LIKE SLOW TIME

"What will the Earth Spirits send me?" Kwame asked Principal Wari.

The smoky pito disappeared.

The principal dusted off his knees as he stood up. "The Earth Spirits are sending you an animal helper just like my monkey, Adoe."

Adoe hopped when he heard his name.

"Animal helpers are powerful . . . and rare," the principal explained. "This means the spirits know how important it is for you to succeed."

5

"What animal will they send me? What powers will it have?" Kwame asked.

The ground rumbled.

"That rumble means your stay-same spell will wear off soon. We don't have time for questions. And speaking of time..." Principal Wari said.

Kwame watched as the principal took a tiny leaf-wrapped hourglass out of his pocket.

"Jai bere," he whispered, and smashed the hourglass on the ground.

Pieces of glass sank into the earth.

Kwame's eyes widened as a white door grew like a tree.

"This door leads to a time loop, Kwame," Principal Wari said. "Time moves much slower there. In our world, we will be in there for two minutes. But four days will pass in the loop. We won't need to eat or sleep. This loop will give us the time we need to prepare you for your mission."

Without another word, the principal stepped through the door and disappeared.

Kwame gulped. *Can I really learn enough magic in four days to save the world?*

He gripped his calabash and entered the time loop, too.

CHAPTER 3

TIME TO TRAIN

Kwame stood in a huge, square room. Each corner held a stone post shaped like an animal—a cheetah, a hawk, a monkey, and a snake. Bookshelves lined the walls.

In the center of the room, Principal Wari sat cross-legged. An hourglass filled with gold sand floated next to him.

8

"Is this the time loop?" Kwame asked, his voice echoing.

"Yes, it's Day One. Let's start," Principal Wari said. "Your Omni calabash can create magic across all four magic types: Earth Breaker, Sun Wielder, Time Bender, and Weather Handler."

Kwame sat down. "Yes. But how do I change types?" he asked.

"Imagine the magic type before casting your spell. Try a Sun Wielder spell. Think of a wall of flames," Principal Wari said.

Kwame pictured it.

"Now say 'Aja fasuo bra,'" the principal said.

"Aja fasuo bra," Kwame repeated.

Whoosh! A single flame shot up from his calabash and disappeared.

Principal Wari nodded. "Again."

"Aja fasuo bra!" Kwame shouted.

WHOOSH! A huge wall of flames shot out of Kwame's calabash, then disappeared.

Principal Wari smiled. "Keeping up the wall will take practice. But this powerful protection spell can burn through anything."

Kwame practiced. The wall of flames always sputtered out.

Just then—*SWISH!* Bright golden sand dropped to the bottom of the hourglass.

"It's Day Two, Kwame. Let's move on," Principal Wari said. He took down a book and opened it in front of Kwame.

"Who are those people?" Kwame asked, pointing to pictures of small people wearing leaf hats.

"These are mmotia," the principal said. "They live in the Secret Forest, which you must cross to reach the Magic Mountain."

11

"How will I find a *secret* forest?" Kwame exclaimed.

Principal Wari flipped to a map. He showed Kwame

the path from the school to the mountain.

Then he taught Kwame all about the forest and mmotia.

Kwame's head spun. *There is so much to remember!*

Principal Wari saw Kwame's worried face. He closed the book and whispered into his calabash.

Two bright-red drinks appeared. They smelled like cranberries.

"Drink this," he said, sipping the drink. "It's called Sobolo."

Kwame drank and immediately felt calmer. "What's in this?" he asked.

"Magical hibiscus leaves. They help you remember," Principal Wari replied.

SWISH! More golden sand dropped.

"It's Day Three now. Let's move on to the saving spell," Principal Wari said. "This is how you will defeat the green flame and rescue Fifi. The spell's power comes from the strength of your friendship."

Kwame nodded.

"Now repeat after me," the principal said. "BRA FIE!"

"BRA FIE!" Kwame shouted. His calabash glowed a bit, but nothing else happened.

"Try again," Principal Wari said. "Think of the times you played with Fifi."

Kwame practiced more. The glow grew brighter but still faded.

SWISH! More sand fell: Day Four had begun.

"BRA FIE!" Kwame shouted with all his might.

Finally, his calabash shook as a golden ray burst from it and shot up to the ceiling.

Principal Wari cheered. "Fantastic work, Kwame! We've completed your training."

Suddenly, Adoe yanked on the principal's hair.

"Ouch!" Principal Wari exclaimed.

CRAACK! CRAACK! CRAACK!

Kwame turned to see three lightning bolts hit the ground in front of him.

CHAPTER 4

TOGETHER AGAIN

Three figures stood before Kwame. His friends, Esi and Papa-Kow, were there! And an advanced-magic student named Baaba was there, too. Kwame, Esi, and Papa-Kow had all started Nkonyaa School together. Baaba had helped them when they first arrived.

Esi and Papa-Kow ran over to Kwame. He squeezed them tight. *If only our friend Fifi was here, too*, Kwame thought.

Baaba turned to Principal Wari. "Esi and Papa-Kow are ready," she said.

"Ah, wonderful," the principal said.

Then Principal Wari looked at Kwame. "Esi the Sun Wielder and Papa-Kow the Weather Handler will join you on your mission. You stand a better chance of getting to the mountain with their help. Baaba and I will stay behind to watch over things here."

"These superstars have been training in a time loop with me," Baaba said. She clapped Papa-Kow's back. "Papa-Kow is amazing with herbs."

Papa-Kow grinned and patted his book of herbs.

"And Esi's magic is now very powerful," Baaba added.

BOOM! The rest of the golden sand fell to the bottom of the hourglass, and the square room disappeared.

Principal Wari pointed at Baaba's bag. "Did you bring the cheetah balls?" he asked.

"Yes," Baaba said, handing one to each student. "You can't use calabash magic to transport yet, so these magic cheetah balls will help you reach the Secret Forest quickly."

The ground rumbled.

"You must hurry," Principal Wari said. "The stay-same spell is wearing off."

"I'm ready!" said Papa-Kow.

"How do we use these?" Esi asked, holding up her cheetah ball.

"Chew and swallow," Baaba told them.

17

Kwame was not sure what cheetah balls would taste like. But when he chewed his, it tasted minty! His feet immediately felt tingly. His tummy felt warm.

"What's happening?!" he yelled.

CHAPTER 5

TRICKSTERS IN THE FOREST

Kwame looked down. His human legs were now cheetah legs! So were Papa-Kow's and Esi's!

"Wow!" Kwame exclaimed, raising a paw.

Principal Wari chuckled. "It feels funny the first time you transform."

He handed Esi a green bag. "This will hold the Boni. Do not touch that calabash."

Esi nodded, putting it in her backpack.

"So what now?" Papa-Kow asked.

Baaba grinned. "Now you run!"

Kwame took a deep breath. *I'm coming, Fifi!*

Kwame started running. He bounced like a spring. He was moving so fast! Papa-Kow and Esi were blurs next to him.

Ahead, he saw a huge forest.

Uh-oh! Principal Wari and Baaba didn't say how to stop! Kwame panicked.

He raised his hands, waiting to hit the trees. But Esi's arm stopped him.

"Woah, Kwame," she said. "We can't enter the Secret Forest without permission."

"Look, we've transformed back," Papa-Kow said, pointing to their feet.

Huge, spiky trees waved in the wind ahead of the trio.

A tiny, annoyed man walked out of the forest. His black clothes and hat were made of leaves. And his feet were turned backward.

A mmotia! Kwame thought.

Esi whispered to her friends, "Black-hat mmotia are friendlier than white-hat mmotia. Papa-Kow also has every mmotia's favorite gift in his backpack."

"*You* are not welcome here!" the black-hat mmotia announced in a deep voice.

Papa-Kow stepped forward with a bunch of bananas. "This is for you," he offered. "Can we please enter this forest?"

The mmotia crossed his arms. "No," he said.

The trees
rustled, and a
mmotia wearing
a white hat came
out. He snatched
the bananas. "Don't
mind Sumaila. I,
Jibril, will take you
through the forest."

"We shouldn't
go with Jibril," Esi
whispered. "White-hat mmotia are very
tricky."

Kwame begged Sumaila. "Please help us!
We need to reach the Magic Mountain in
time to stop the green flame."

Sumaila frowned. "That evil flame has
already destroyed parts of our forest. Only
an Omni calabash can stop him. And the
flame holds the only Omni!"

Kwame took out his calabash.

Sumaila's eyes widened when he saw the symbols on it. "How did *you* get an Omni?"

Kwame shrugged shyly.

"Fine, follow me," Sumaila said grumpily. "But don't touch anything. If you do, the forest will swallow you up forever."

Kwame shivered as the spiky trees opened for them to enter.

CHAPTER 6

DON'T TOUCH!

It was dark and smoky inside the Secret Forest. Tall, spiky trees blocked the sunlight.

Esi spoke a spell into her calabash, and it lit up.

Papa-Kow groaned as he looked around. "These trees are broken!"

Esi pointed. "This grass is burnt black!"

And Kwame coughed. "There is thick smoke everywhere."

"The green flame did all this damage." Sumaila sighed.

The ground rumbled.

"We're running out of time," said Kwame.

Esi squeezed his hand. "We must hurry!"

Kwame nodded.

Papa-Kow lagged behind the others. He had his herb book out and kept excitedly pointing to herbs. "I see Dammabo! There's Okyem!"

"Keep up, Papa-Kow!" Kwame called out. "And remember, don't touch anything!"

"I'm being careful," Papa-Kow replied.

They walked a bit farther, until they reached a clearing.

Nyahaha! An evil voice laughed.

"That's Jibril's laugh!" Sumaila exclaimed.

"Stay close, everybody!" Esi yelled.

Kwame stood back-to-back with Esi and Sumaila, but Papa-Kow was gone!

Jibril's singsong voice echoed through the trees. "I showed your friend an herb he couldn't resist touching. He is mine now."

Esi pointed. "Oh no!"

Kwame looked back and saw Papa-Kow wrapped in vines. His eyes were closed.

Esi raced over to help Papa-Kow.

"Don't!" Sumaila shouted.

But it was too late. Esi touched the vines!

She fainted as vines covered her, too. The light went out in her calabash after it fell to the ground.

"I told you all not to touch anything!" Sumaila said.

"Please help them!" Kwame cried.

Sumaila shook his head. "I can't. Forest rules ban me from interfering with its magic."

Nyahaha! Jibril's cackling grew louder.

Kwame felt like he had swallowed a rock. *I can't touch the vines trapping Papa-Kow and Esi . . . How can I save them?!*

CHAPTER 7

BANANAS

Kwame thought back to his training. He remembered that mmotia loved bananas. So he spoke an Earth Breaker spell into his calabash. "Akwadu bra."

Six bunches of bananas appeared.

Kwame shouted into the darkness. "Jibril, please let my friends go! You can have these bananas!"

Nyahaha! cackled Jibril as he stepped out of the trees.

Then he stomped on the bananas. "I don't need your bananas. I'm going to give these two humans to Bonsam. Then he will give me enough bananas to last forever!"

"Who's Bonsam?" Kwame asked.

Sumaila groaned. "Bonsam rules the forest. His magic is very strong! You can't let Jibril take your friends to him."

"But what can I do?" Kwame replied.

Sumaila looked him in the eyes. "If only there was a powerful calabash that could burn the vines off without burning your friends, too."

-BONSAM-

That's it! I'll try casting the Sun Wielder wall spell! Kwame thought. He imagined a flame. And just as Jibril reached for Papa-Kow and Esi, Kwame shouted, "AJA FASUO BRA!"

CHAPTER 8

THE ESCAPE

A huge wall of flames burst from Kwame's calabash. It circled Kwame and his friends. Smaller flames leaped onto the vines and burned them off of Esi and Papa-Kow.

Jibril jumped back.

"Good work!" Sumaila said to Kwame. "Now grab your friends and follow me!"

Kwame raced to Esi and Papa-Kow. They awoke as if from a deep sleep.

"Let's go!" Kwame shouted.

He helped Esi and Papa-Kow stand up, and together they raced after Sumaila.

The black-hatted mmotia led them to the edge of the trees. Then he pushed the three friends out of the forest. "Don't come back!" Sumaila yelled.

Kwame turned around to thank Sumaila, but the Secret Forest was gone! And in front of him was the path to the Magic Mountain.

Esi and Papa-Kow sat on the ground.

"What happened back there?" Esi asked.

"Papa-Kow touched an herb, and the forest's magic took him. Then you went to save him, Esi. But because you touched the vines, the magic got you, too," Kwame explained.

"Sorry, I couldn't help myself," Papa-Kow mumbled. "But I did put this rare herb in my backpack before the vines grabbed me." He showed his friends  the plant. "This is Sabi Sabi. It hasn't been seen for hundreds of years!"

Suddenly, Esi patted herself in panic. "Oh no! My calabash! It's gone!" She sank to the ground.

Kwame and Papa-Kow knelt beside her.

"I'm really sorry, Esi. This is all my fault," Papa-Kow said.

"I know you didn't mean any harm." She wiped tears from her eyes. "But now I can't do magic."

Kwame hugged her. "I'm sure Principal Wari will know how to get your calabash back."

"I hope you're right." Esi sniffled.

Kwame stood up. "Let's keep moving."

The three friends followed the hilly road.

Soon Kwame smelled salt water. When he turned a corner, he gasped. "There's a rainbow-colored sea in the middle of the road! Principal Wari didn't mention this . . ."

Esi and Papa-Kow stopped, too.

"How will we get across?" Esi asked.

"It's too far to swim," Papa-Kow replied.

"And we don't have a boat," Esi added.

"Know any flying spells?" Kwame asked.

His friends shook their heads.

Kwame looked at the setting sun. "Well, let's get some rest." He tried to smile. "We'll figure this out tomorrow."

Papa-Kow cast a spell to make dinner. Kwame cast one to make a tent.

Then they all huddled in for the night.

Kwame kept his eyes on the top of the Magic Mountain. *I'm coming Fifi!* he thought as he drifted off to sleep.

CHAPTER 9

THE DREAM

Kwame was standing outside his classroom at Nkonyaa School. Fifi stood across from him, holding the Boni calabash. Their teacher, Ms. Kumi, was nearby.

"Fifi, drop that calabash!" she shouted.

Fifi's voice sounded deep and growly. He looked like a monster with green, hairy skin and sharp teeth. "No one will be mean to me again!"

37

He pointed a finger at
Ms. Kumi. A green bolt
turned her into a puddle.

Kwame shouted, "Fifi,
stop!"

Fifi turned to Kwame
and growled, "Bo no."

A green bolt headed
toward Kwame!
Kwame held up his
calabash and—he
wasn't turned into a

puddle. But his calabash was shaking! And
inside it, a green whirlpool swirled.

Suddenly, Kwame was on a mountainside,
surrounded by thick, green mist. He could
hear Fifi shouting for help. He followed the
voice up the mountain.

When he got to the top, a big green bolt
headed straight for him!

His heart raced. Kwame sat up in the tent. *That was only a dream?!*

He crawled outside. It was almost morning.

How will we get to Fifi with this rainbow sea in the way? He threw a small rock into the water.

"Oi!" a tiny voice cried out. "Watch where you're throwing rocks!"

CHAPTER 10

FISHY BUSINESS

A fish swam up to the beach. "Who throws rocks at fish?" he grumbled, rubbing his brown head.

Kwame's mouth fell open. *A talking fish!* "I—I'm sorry I hit you," he said.

"I bet you are! The name's Venyo. So why are you throwing rocks?" the fish asked.

40

"I'm Kwame. I only threw that rock because I'm upset. It's very important that my friends and I get to the Magic Mountain," Kwame said, pointing. "But this sea is in the way. We can't cross it."

"Ah, yes. This sea appears once every two hundred years," Venyo said.

Kwame snapped his fingers. "That's why it wasn't on the map!"

"Only Mami Wata, the queen of the sea, can grant you safe passage," Venyo explained.

"She can?" replied Kwame.

"Yes. But she always asks for something in return," Venyo warned.

"Wait a second," Kwame said. He ran to wake Papa-Kow and Esi.

Kwame told them what Venyo had said.

"Can we trust a talking fish?" Papa-Kow asked.

"We don't have a choice." Esi shrugged.

The three 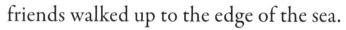 friends walked up to the edge of the sea.

"Let me guess," Venyo said. "You want to see the queen?"

They nodded.

"Alright, wait here." The fish disappeared beneath the waves.

After a few minutes, Venyo was back—with a waterspout roaring behind him! "Get in!" he shouted over the noise.

Kwame and his friends stepped in.

"Oh!" Kwame said. "How strange! The water doesn't feel wet!"

"And the bottom feels firm!" Papa-Kow added.

"Time to go under!" Venyo shouted.

"Wait! How will we breathe underwater?" asked Esi.

"Don't worry. Here we go!" Venyo said. He waved his fin.

Suddenly, the waterspout spun faster. Kwame, Esi, and Papa-Kow all disappeared under the water. *FIZZZZZ!*

CHAPTER 11
THE QUEEN OF THE SEA

Kwame's eyes widened. "We are underwater," he said to Papa-Kow and Esi.

A round, squishy bubble had formed around each of their heads. Fish swam above them. They floated down into a huge hall with shining seashell walls that glittered like jewels. There were statues all around.

"Wow!" Esi exclaimed.

In front of them, a smiling woman sat on the throne. She was dressed in gold, with a rainbow-colored snake around her neck. Long locs flowed past her tail fins. Next to her were octopus guards holding spears.

"Kneel!" the guards thundered.

The trio knelt as the queen spoke. Her soft voice filled the hall like a harp. "Welcome, humans. I am Mami Wata. I can help you cross my beautiful rainbow sea. But first, where is my gift?"

Kwame's heart jumped. "Umm, we don't have one."

The queen's smile disappeared. "You ask for passage without a gift?!" she shouted.

The guards banged their spears on the ground. *THUMP! THUMP!*

Mami Wata took a deep breath. "Well then, you will have to play my game."

"A game?" Kwame asked.

"Yes. You must each answer one riddle," the queen explained. "If two of you answer correctly, you win and I will help you all cross my sea."

"What happens if we lose?" Papa-Kow questioned.

An evil grin spread across Mami Wata's face. "You will become my statues!"

We could get stuck here forever, Kwame thought. He whispered to his friends, "What should we do?"

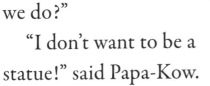

"I don't want to be a statue!" said Papa-Kow.

Esi looked unsure. "I don't know a lot of riddles," she said.

Kwame sighed. "But Fifi needs our help . . ."

They looked at one another, then nodded.

"Okay," Kwame told Mami Wata. "We will play your game."

CHAPTER 12
RIDDLE ME

The trio stood side by side in Mami Wata's great hall. Kwame's heart pounded. *We only need to answer two riddles correctly*, he thought.

"Who will go first?" the queen demanded.

Esi stepped forward. "I will."

Mami Wata closed her eyes, thinking. Then she spoke. "What do you call a water pot that hangs in the sky?"

Esi frowned.

"Answer me!" Mami Wata demanded.

Kwame held his breath. *I don't think Esi knows the answer, but I don't either*, he thought.

Finally, Esi shook her head.

"Seize her!" The queen pointed at Esi.

Two guards grabbed Esi and took her aside.

Mami Wata glared at Papa-Kow and Kwame. "Ha! No human has ever guessed one of my riddles!" she bragged. "Who's next?"

Papa-Kow shivered. "I am."

"Here is your riddle," Mami Wata said. "I know lots of things and can teach without speaking. What am I?"

Papa-Kow bit his lip, thinking hard.

"Well?" Mami Wata asked.

Papa-Kow smiled. "A book."

Mami Wata's snake hissed.

"How did a human answer correctly?!" The queen turned to Kwame with a mean look in her eye. "But YOU won't know 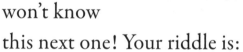 this next one! Your riddle is: I have teeth but I cannot bite. What am I?"

Kwame thought hard.

Mami Wata rose from her throne. "You don't have an answer! Time for you three to become statutes! I have the perfect place for you!"

Kwame quickly responded, "The answer is a comb."

Mami Wata shrieked. "*Kids* solved two of my riddles?!" She glared at them. "Fine. I grant you passage. But don't come back!"

The guards let Esi go, and the waterspout reappeared. It spun around the trio. *FIZZ!!!*

This time, the waterspout shot them up into the sky. Soon, it set Kwame and his friends down on a sandy beach at the foot of the Magic Mountain.

"We're finally here!" Kwame cheered.

But at that moment, the ground rumbled, and an ear-splitting roar filled the air—*RAAAWWWRRR!*

Kwame looked up to see a green mist speeding down the mountain toward them!

THE MIST

The green mist covered the beach like thick soup. Kwame couldn't see his friends. He shouted, "Esi! Papa-Kow! Where are you?"

Kwame could hear their voices, but he couldn't tell where they were coming from. It sounded like they were speaking through a pillow.

Just then, a new voice pierced through the mist. "Kwame, help!"

Fifi! Kwame thought. *This is just like my dream!*

Kwame heard the voice again. "Kwame! Help me, please!"

I need to save Fifi! Kwame thought. He felt scared, but his friend was in trouble.

Kwame raced forward, following the voice. He scrambled up the mountain path, waving his hands in front of him. The mist was so thick, he had to be careful not to bump into things.

"Kwame! Help!" Fifi's voice grew louder the higher Kwame climbed.

Finally, Kwame burst through the edge of the mist. He was on top of the mountain, and right in front of him was the back of the green flame!

CHAPTER 14

THE MEETING

Kwame froze. He noticed Okomfo Anochi's Omni calabash and the Boni calabash next to the green flame. Each calabash rested on a mound of clay. Pots and bottles filled with leaves and liquids were lined up around the calabashes.

The green flame is preparing to cast the spell the principal warned me about! Kwame thought. He shouted, "Fifi, I'm here!"

The green flame turned and growled, "Fifi is gone! I tricked you into coming alone—so I could destroy *your* Omni calabash. It's the only thing that can stop me."

Kwame took a step back.

The green flame pointed at Kwame. "BO NO!" it yelled.

That's the puddle spell! Kwame remembered, jumping out of the way.

A bright-green bolt dissolved a rock right where he had been standing.

I need to do the saving spell now! Kwame sat down and closed his eyes. He thought of the times he and Fifi had played Oware together. Then he shouted, "BRA FIE!!!"

A golden bolt leaped out of his calabash and hit the green flame. The flame wobbled.

Kwame watched, holding his breath. *Did my spell work?!*

After a moment, the green flame roared. "Your magic is not powerful enough to stop me! Now I will destroy your calabash!"

The flame pointed at Kwame again. "BO NO!"

Kwame remembered how his calabash had saved him from the green bolt before. So he held it up in front of him again.

BRAAAM! The green bolt hit Kwame's calabash.

The Omni vibrated in his hands, but Kwame held on tightly. *I can't let go!* he thought.

Suddenly—

CRACK!

Kwame looked down in horror. His calabash had split in two! *I can't cast the saving spell without my calabash! Now there's no way to save Fifi!*

The green flame cackled. "Ha! Now that I've destroyed your Omni, *nothing* can stop me from becoming all-powerful! BO NO!!"

Another massive green bolt headed toward Kwame.

CHAPTER 15

PUDDLES

At that moment, Papa-Kow and Esi burst out of the mist and into the clearing. Esi saw the bolt heading toward Kwame. She pushed him out of the way, and it hit the mountainside.

BRAAM!

"Did you cast the saving spell?" Papa-Kow asked Kwame.

"I tried, but the spell didn't work!" Kwame replied. "And now my calabash is broken." He showed it to them.

The green flame floated closer to the trio. "BO NO!" it yelled as another bolt headed toward the three friends.

"Papa-Kow! Protection Spell!" cried Esi.

Papa-Kow nodded and shouted into his calabash. "Mmframa bra!"

A whirlwind whooshed out of his calabash and blew the green bolt away.

The green flame shrieked again. "BO NO!" it yelled, pointing at Papa-Kow and Esi.

Two green bolts zoomed toward them. They both cried out as they dissolved into puddles.

"NOOO!" Kwame screamed.

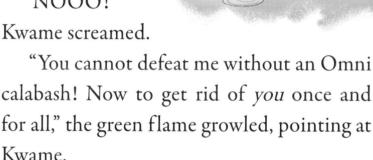

"You cannot defeat me without an Omni calabash! Now to get rid of *you* once and for all," the green flame growled, pointing at Kwame.

Out of the corner of his eye, Kwame spotted Okomfo Anochi's Omni calabash on the clay mound. *That Omni is my only chance to save the world!*

He leaped toward the calabash as the flame screamed, "BO NO!"

Two green bolts headed his way.

As soon as Kwame touched the Omni calabash, a burst of power filled him. His whole body vibrated. His tummy felt like a thousand bees were buzzing inside it. *Oh no!* he thought. *Something is wrong!*

CHAPTER 16

OKOMFO ANOCHI

The two green bolts froze and a bright light flashed as time stopped.

A tall man walked toward Kwame. He had an Akrafena sword tied to his back, and a hawk sat on his shoulder.

Okomfo Anochi! Kwame thought. *The first and most powerful Nkonyaa elder. He taught me about my calabash.*

Okomfo stood next to him and said, "My calabash is yours to use."

Then Kwame heard a voice in his head. Somehow, he knew it belonged to the hawk. The voice was deep but kind. *I am your animal helper sent by the Earth Spirits. My name is Quainoo. I will lend you my power.*

The hawk flew off Okomfo's shoulder and landed on Kwame's. Immediately, Kwame felt Quainoo's power flood through him. His body vibrated with power, and his vision blurred.

Okomfo disappeared, and time started up again.

The two green bolts were speeding toward Kwame. But this time, he didn't feel afraid.

Kwame gripped the Omni calabash. He knew he had to do the saving spell again. He closed his eyes. He thought of when he and Fifi had stayed up late reading. He thought of Fifi bringing him a chocolate bar to cheer him up. He remembered how they had shared it. Kwame felt the warmth of those memories flow into the calabash.

Kwame heard Quainoo's voice in his head:
You're ready, Kwame. Now!

"BRA FIE!" Kwame shouted.

A golden wave rushed out of the calabash!
It swallowed the green bolts.

Then—

"NOOOOOOO!! Not possible!!!" the
green flame shrieked as it got sucked in as
well!

CHAPTER 17

GREEN SLIME

All that was left of the flame was a pool of green slime. Kwame walked over to it. *Did my saving spell work? Where's Fifi?* he worried.

Just then, the slime began bubbling and a green blob rose out of it.

Kwame stepped back, holding his breath. As he watched, the blob transformed . . .

A smaller boy with wild hair shaped like a flame staggered out of the slime.

Tears filled Kwame's eyes. "Fifi!" He rushed over to his friend.

Fifi shook his head, confused. "Where am I? Kwame, why aren't we at school?"

Kwame explained what had happened.

Fifi's mouth opened in shock. "I don't remember anything after I first touched the Boni calabash! What have I done?!" He held his head in his hands.

Kwame hugged his friend. "You didn't do those awful things. The green flame did."

Just then, they heard more soft bubbling sounds. The puddles of Esi and Papa-Kow were both puffing out purple smoke. Kwame noticed the mist around the mountaintop vanishing, too.

"With the green flame gone, all of its evil magic is disappearing!" Kwame exclaimed.

Esi and Papa-Kow stepped out of the smoke. They were wobbly on their feet.

"That felt weird," Esi said.

When Esi and Papa-Kow saw Fifi, they raced to hug their friend.

"Fifi! It's so good to see you!" Papa-Kow cheered.

Then Esi saw the hawk flying near Kwame. "Who's that?!" she exclaimed.

Kwame smiled. "Meet Quainoo! He's my animal helper."

Quainoo bowed his head in greeting.

Suddenly, there was a mighty *CRACK!* The friends jumped back as the ground split open right beside them!

Oh no, Kwame thought. *The stay-same spell's magic has run out!*

"Hurry!" he yelled to his friends. "We need to get the Boni and Omni calabashes back to the shrine! We still need to stop the world from falling apart!"

CHAPTER 18

HOMEWARD

The four friends stood on top of the Magic Mountain. The ground rumbled under their feet.

"We need to return the calabashes *now*!" Papa-Kow said.

"But how will we get back to school from here?" Esi asked.

Fifi piped up. "I have an idea." He pointed to Okomfo's Omni calabash. "That calabash can get us home. I read about a transportation spell in an ancient spell book."

"Great," Esi said. "Tell Kwame the spell while I grab the Boni calabash!"

Esi pulled out the special bag Principal Wari had given her.

"Remember, Esi: Principal Wari said not to touch that calabash, or *you'll* turn into the green flame," Papa-Kow warned.

Esi carefully wrapped the Boni calabash.

She also picked up the pieces of Kwame's broken calabash.

Kwame gripped Okomfo's calabash with both hands. Then he took a deep breath and shouted the spell Fifi taught him: "FA YEN KO SUKU!!"

HUMMMMMMMM! Kwame heard a high-pitched hum as he and his friends disappeared in a puff of golden smoke.

CHAPTER 19

SCHOOL SWEET SCHOOL

Kwame, Fifi, Esi, and Papa-Kow appeared back at Nkonyaa School. They were near the shrine where the two special calabashes belonged. The sky was dark with storm clouds. Lightning flashed and the ground rumbled.

Kwame could see that the school building was shaking. Bits of it were falling off! Nkonyaa elders were running with the students, away from the school.

Principal Wari ran over. He smiled when he saw Fifi. "You are all just in time," he said, rushing them into the shrine. "And Kwame, I see that you have a new friend." He winked at Quainoo.

The principal directed Esi. "Put the Boni calabash on its pedestal. But be careful."

Kwame watched his friend unwrap the green calabash and place it back where it belonged. As soon as she did, the rumbling stopped.

Principal Wari smiled. "You have stopped the crumbling just in time. Now, Kwame, put the Omni calabash on its pedestal so that the damage that's been done can be repaired."

Kwame lifted Okomfo's Omni calabash to put it back on its pedestal. But it floated in the air and wouldn't set down.

Principal Wari tried to touch the calabash, but it zapped him. "Ow," he said.

Kwame took a step back and the calabash followed him.

The principal scratched his beard. "Hmm. Very interesting. Okomfo's calabash seems somehow connected to you now."

Suddenly, Esi pointed out the window. "Look!"

CHAPTER 20
THE NKONYAA TREE

Outside, the dark storm clouds had turned white. It was pouring golden rain!

Principal Wari chuckled. "Ha! This magic rain will undo the damage the Boni did." He patted Kwame's shoulder. "How does it feel to have saved the world?"

Kwame was smiling so hard his cheeks hurt. "I had help," he said, looking over at his friends.

Esi remembered Kwame's broken calabash at that moment. She showed the pieces to Principal Wari.

The principal's eyes widened.

"Can my Omni be fixed?" Kwame asked.

Principal Wari examined it. "I believe so. And perhaps, when it is fixed, Okomfo's Omni will go back to its pedestal."

Principal Wari turned to Fifi next. "Young man, you certainly caused a lot of trouble."

Fifi looked up at the principal. "I'm *really* sorry for stealing the Boni. I just wanted to scare those older students so they'd stop being mean to me. I didn't mean to use it."

Principal Wari had a kind look on his face. "I understand why you did what you did, Fifi. But using magic you aren't ready for is dangerous. And hurting people who hurt you is never the  answer. Promise that won't happen again?"

Fifi nodded.

"Principal Wari, we only made it back here in time because of Fifi," Kwame added. "He taught me a spell from an ancient spell book."

"Well done, Fifi! You're better at magic than most older students," the principal said. "They can't read ancient spell books!"

Fifi and Kwame grinned at each other.

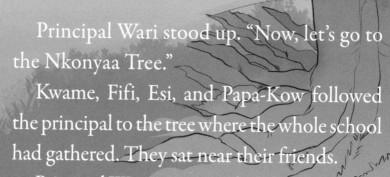

Principal Wari stood up. "Now, let's go to the Nkonyaa Tree."

Kwame, Fifi, Esi, and Papa-Kow followed the principal to the tree where the whole school had gathered. They sat near their friends.

Principal Wari announced, "Thanks to these four brave students, especially Kwame, the world is not crumbling anymore!"

Everyone cheered. Principal Wari tapped his calabash and a feast appeared.

Kwame couldn't believe his eyes. The picnic blanket was full of his favorite foods!

Esi touched the principal's sleeve. "Umm, I'm not sure I belong here anymore," she whispered, with tears in her eyes. "I lost my calabash in the Secret Forest."

Principal Wari put a hand on her shoulder. "Don't worry," he said. "The Nkonyaa Tree will return your calabash."

Esi brightened. "Really?"

Principal Wari held his calabash in one hand and touched the tree with the other. Then he said, "Fa san bra."

Kwame watched the tree. Its candy cane–striped leaves whispered in the wind. But nothing happened. "Why isn't the tree returning Esi's calabash?" he asked. "I thought magic everywhere was back to normal now."

The principal looked serious. "It seems the tree's magic has not been restored. Without this magical tree, there will be no new calabashes—and no one new will be able to learn magic. Soon, all our calabashes will also lose their magic!"

Without calabash magic, Nkonyaa School would have to close, Kwame thought.

Just then, Fifi yelled, "Kwame, your robe!"

Everyone gasped.

Kwame looked down. The symbol on his robe was changing!

DID YOU KNOW?

Kwame's Magic Quest is inspired by African cultures. Ghana, a country in West Africa, is where this story takes place.

AFRICA

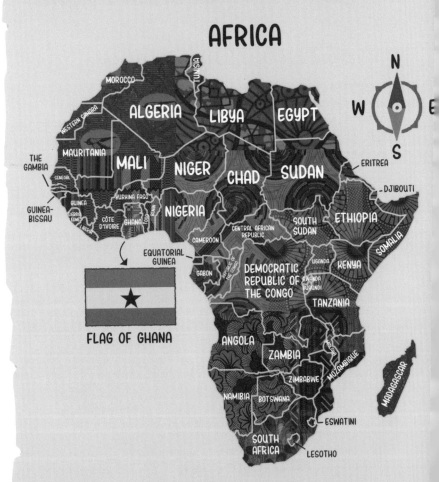

FLAG OF GHANA

There are three magical creatures in this book that come straight from traditional Ghanaian beliefs!

1. Mmotia are believed to be tricksters with magical powers that live in the forest.

2. Mami Wata is known as the queen of the sea in many countries both inside and outside Africa. Nigeria, Togo, Brazil, and Haiti are a few. Beautiful and powerful, she is often seen as a mermaid who protects those who respect her.

3. Bonsam is short for "Sasabonsam"—an evil, tall, hairy, wild-eyed monster that sits high up on "odum" *(Milicia regia)* trees. He tries to capture people who get too close, and he rules over some mmotia.

In many African cultures, magic users typically have an animal helper who assists them in doing magic and connects them to the spirit world. Kwame's hawk is based on a long-crested eagle, a real bird native to Ghana.

As you read this series, you will learn about Ghanaian and African cultures—and, of course, magic!

LEARN MORE!

Pito: A traditional drink for adults in Ghana. It is sometimes poured on the ground during magic ceremonies or drank as a way to honor ancestors.

Twi (chwee): Twi is a language spoken in Ghana. "Mmotia" is a Twi word. "Amotia" is the plural of "mmotia," but the author chose to use "mmotia" as both the singular and plural word. All the magic spells in this book use real Twi words! Here's one spell and its meaning:

> ✦ **Jai bere (jai breh):** Jai (real spelling Gyae) means "stop." And "bere" (real spelling berɛ) means "time." So together it means "stop time."

School robes: The robes in the book are a mix of Kente (a cloth with special meanings made from colorful threads) and Batakari (traditional clothes first worn by the Hausa and Frafra people in northern Ghana, but popular today across the nation).

Herbs: Dammabo and Okyem are real herbs used in Ghana for traditional medicine!

Riddles: These are important in African cultures to teach lessons and wisdom. The three riddles in the book are real riddles from Ghana! (Did you guess Mami Wata's first riddle? A coconut hangs in the air, and when you crack it open, you find water inside.)

ABOUT THE CREATORS

BERNARD MENSAH grew up in Ghana, where he spent his days climbing trees, playing soccer, or dreaming up stories at the library.

Bernard now lives in the United Kingdom with his family, where he works with computers and writes stories. He wishes he could have an Omni calabash like Kwame!

Bernard writes children's books for all ages.

NATASHA NAYO is from Ghana, where she lives today.

She graduated from the Maryland Institute College of Art with a BFA in Animation and Illustration. Natasha loves creating artwork that makes her audience smile. And she wants to help pave the way for other African-born artists aiming to get into the publishing industry.

Kwame's Magic Quest is Natasha's first children's book series.

QUESTIONS & ACTIVITIES

✦ **P**rincipal Wari casts a time spell in Chapter Two. How much time passes in real life? How much time passes in the time loop?

✦ **K**wame, Esi, and Papa-Kow travel underwater by way of a magical waterspout. Research what a waterspout is in real life.

✦ **K**wame's animal helper, Quainoo, is a hawk. What do you know about hawks in real life? What do you think Quainoo's special powers might be?

✦ **T**he Omni calabash refuses to go back to its pedestal in the end. Why do you think this is?

✦ **I**magine you are a student at Nkonyaa School. What kind of calabash do you have? Draw your calabash and label its powers.